*Snow in the Desert* was first published in the collection entitled *The Gabble – And Other Stories* by Neal Asher. First published in 2008 by Tor, an imprint of Pan Macmillan, a division of Macmillan Publishers International Limited.

Copyright © Neal Asher 2008
All rights reserved.

This edition published in 2024
by BOTH Publishing

The author asserts their moral right to be identified as the author of their work, in accordance with the Copyright, Designs and Patents Act, 1988.

This book is sold subject to the condition that no part may be reproduced, distributed, or transmitted in any form or by any means, including photocopying, recording, or other electronic or mechanical methods, without the prior written permission of the publisher.

A CIP catalogue record of this book is available from the British Library

ISBN - 978-1-913603-42-7
eBook available - ISBN - 978-1-913603-43-4

Printed by Ingram Spark.
Distributed by BOTH Publishing.

Cover design by Chrissey Harrison & Alistair Sims.
Original artwork by Jackie Burns.
Typeset by Chrissey Harrison.

Part of the Dyslexic Friendly Quick Reads Project.

# www.booksonthehill.co.uk

# SNOW IN THE
# DESERT

## Neal Asher

**Other dyslexic friendly quick read titles from BOTH publishing**

Six Lights Off Green Scar

The Breath

The House on the Old Cliffs

The Clockwork Eyeball

Stamp of a Criminal

Sharpe's Skirmish

Blood Toll

Silver for Silence

Sherlock Holmes and the Four Kings of Sweden

# Snow in the Desert

A sand shark broke through the top face of the dune only to be snatched by a crab-bird and shredded in mid-air. Hirald squatted down, turned on her chameleonwear and faded into the violet sand, only her Toshiba goggles and the blunt snout of her singun visible. The crab-bird was a small one, but she had quickly learnt never to underestimate them. If the prey was too large for one to take, it would take pieces instead. No motile source of protein was too large to attack. The shame was that all the lifeforms on Vatch were based on left-helix proteins, so to a crab-bird human flesh was completely without nourishment. The birds did not know this and just became irritable as their hunger increased. The circle was vicious.

The bird stripped the shark of its blade-legs and armoured mandibles and flew off with the bleeding and writhing torso, probably to feed to its chick. Hirald stood up and faded back into existence; a tall woman in a tight-fitting body suit webbed with cooling veins and hung with insulated pockets. On her back she carried a desert survival pack, for the look of things. The singun went into a button-down holster that looked as if it might hold only a simple projectile weapon, not the formidable device it did hold. She removed her goggles, mask and hat, and tucked them away in one of her many pockets before moving on across the sand. Her thin features, blue eyes and long blonde hair were exposed to oven temperatures and skin-flaying ultraviolet. Such had been the way of things for many weeks now. Occasionally she drank some water; a matter of form, just in case anyone was watching.

He was called, inevitably, Snow, but with his plastron mask and dust robes it was not immediately evident he was an albino. The mask, made from the shell of an Earth-import terrapin, was what identified him to those who knew of him – that, and his tendency to leave corpses behind him. At last count the reward for his stasis-preserved testicles was twenty thousand shillings, or the equivalent value in precious metals like copper or manganese. Many people had tried for the reward and their epitaph was just that: they had tried. Three people at the water station, on the edge of the Menilar flat, were waiting to try. They had weapons, strength and skill, balanced against the crippling honour code of the Andronache. Snow had all the former and no honour code. Born on Earth so long ago even he doubted his memories of the time, he had long since dispensed with anything that might get in the way of plain survival. Morality, he often argued, is a purely human invention only to be indulged in times of plenty. Another of his little aphorisms ran something along the lines of: if you're up shit creek without a paddle, don't expect the coast guard. His contemporaries on Vatch never knew what to make of that one, but then Vatchians had no use for words like creek, coast or paddle.

The water station was an ovoid of metal mounted ten metres above the ground on a forest of scaffolding. Nailing it to the ground was the silvery tube of the geothermal energy tap that provided the power for the transmuter; the reason it was possible for humans to exist on this practically waterless planet. The transmuter took complex compounds, stripped them of their elementary hydrogen, and combined that with the abundant oxygen given off by the dryform algae that turned all the sands of Vatch to violet. Water was the product, but there were many interesting by-products; strange metals and silica compounds were one of the planet's main exports.

As he topped the final dune Snow raised his image-intensifier to his eyes and scanned ahead. The station was in reality a small city, the centre of commerce, the centre of life. Under his mask he frowned to himself. He did not know about the three men specifically, but he knew their type would be there. Unfortunately he needed water to take him on the last stage of his journey and this was the only place. A confrontation was inevitable.

Snow strode down the face of the dune and onto a dusty track snaking towards the station. At the side of the road a water thief lay dying at the bottom of a condensation jar. He scratched at the hot glass with blistered fingers as Snow passed, but Snow ignored him. It was harsh punishment, but how else to treat someone who regarded his fellow human beings as no more than walking water barrels? As he drew nearer to the station the cries of the hawkers and stallholders in the ground city reached out to him, like the chorus from a rookery, and he could see the buzz of activity in the scaffold maze. Soon he entered the ground city and its noisy life, soon after, his presence was noted and reported. By the time he passed through the moisture lock of the Sand House – a ubiquitous name for hostelries – and was taking off his mask in the cool interior, the three killers were buckling on their weapons and offering prayers to their various family gods.

"My pardon, master. I must see your tag. The Androche herself has declared the law enforceable by a two-month branding. The word is that too many outlaws now survive on the fringe." The waiter could not help staring at Snow's pink eyes and bloodless face.

"No problem, friend," said Snow, and after fumbling through his robes produced his micro-etched identity tag and handed it over. The waiter glanced at the briefly revealed leather-clad stump that terminated Snow's left arm and pretended not to notice. He put the tag through his portable reader and was much relieved when no alarm sounded. Snow was well aware that not everyone was checked like this, only the more suspicious-looking customers, like himself.

"What would you like, master?"

"A litre of chilled lager," said Snow.

The waiter looked at him doubtfully.

"Which I will pay for now," said Snow, handing over a ten-shilling note. The waiter looked alarmed by such a large sum in cash money and hurried off with it as quickly as he could. When he came back with a litre of lager in a thermos stein with combination-locked top, many eyes followed his progress. Here was an indication of wealth. Snow would not have agreed with this. He had worked it out. A litre of water would only have cost two shillings less, and the water lost through sweat evaporation little different. Two shillings, plus a little, for imbibing fluid in a much more pleasant form. He had nearly finished his litre and was relishing the sheer cellular pleasure of rehydration when the three entered the Sand House. He recognized them for what they were almost immediately. Before paying the slightest attention to them he drained every last drop of lager from the frictionless vessel.

"You are Snow, the albino," said the first, standing before his table. Snow observed her and felt a gnawing depression. Even after all these years he could not shake an aversion to killing women, or in this case girls. She could not have been more than twenty. She stood before him attired in monofilament coveralls and weapons harness. Her face was elfin under a head of cropped black hair spiked out with gold-fleck grease.

"No, I'm not," he said, and turned his attention elsewhere.

"Don't fuck with me," she said with a tiredness that was beyond her years. "I know who you are. You are an albino and your left hand is missing." He returned his attention to her.

"My name is Jelda Conley. People call me Whitey. I have often been confused with this Snow you refer to and it was on one such occasion that I lost my hand. Now please leave me alone."

The girl stepped back, confused. The Andronache honour code did not allow for creative lying. Snow glanced past her and noted one of her companions speaking to the owner who had sent the nervous waiter over. The lies would not be enough. He watched while the owner called over the waiter and checked the screen of his tag reader. The companion approached the girl, whispered in her ear.

"You lied to me," she said.

"No I didn't," said Snow.

"Yes you did!"

This was getting ridiculous. Snow stared off into the distance and ignored her.

"I challenge you," said the girl.

There, it was said. Snow pretended he had not heard her.

"I said I challenge you."

By the code she could now kill him. It was against the law but accepted practice. Snow felt a sinking sensation as she stepped back.

"Stand and face me, coward."

With a tiredness that was wholly genuine Snow rose to his feet. She snatched her slammer. Snow reacted. She hit the floor on her back with the front of her monofilament coverall breaking down and a smoking hole between her pert little breasts. Snow stepped past the table, past her, strode to the moisture lock, vomit held back by clenched teeth. Hoping the whole thing had been too fast for anyone to be sure of the weapon he had used.

It rested on the violet sands at the edge of a spaceport, which was strewn with huge flying-wing shuttles, outbuildings and hangars. It stood between the spaceport and the sprawl of Vatchian buildings linked by moisture-sealed walkways and the glass domes that covered the incongruous green of the parks. And in no way did it resemble any of the constructs around it. It was standard; to be found on a thousand planets of the human Polity, and it was the reason the expansion of the human race beggared the imagination. The runcible facility was a mirrored sphere fifty metres across, seemingly prevented from rolling away by the two L-shaped constructs of the buffers on either side of it. All around it, the glass-roofed embarkation lounges; a puddle of light. Within, the Skaidon gate performed its miracle every few minutes; bringing in quince, mitter travellers, from all across the Polity, and sending them away again.

Beck stood back from the arrivals entrance and watched the twin horns of the runcible on its dais of black glass. He watched the shimmer of the cusp between and impatiently checked his watch, not that they would be late, or early. They would arrive on time to the nanosecond. The runcible AI saw to that. Precisely on time a man stepped through the shimmer, a woman, another man, another woman. They matched the descriptions he had been given, and his greeting was effusive as they came through into the lounge.

"Your transport awaits outside," he told them, hurrying them to exit. The Merchant did not want them to stay in the city. He wanted them out, those were Beck's instructions, amongst others. Once they were in the hover transport the man Beck took to be the leader caught hold of his shoulder.

"The weapons," he said.

"Not here, not here," said Beck nervously, and took the transport out of the city.

Out on the sand Beck brought the transport down and as the four climbed out he pulled a large case from the back of the transport. He was sweating, and not just because of the heat.

"Here," he said, and opened the case.

The man reached inside and took out a small shiny pistol, snub-nosed and deadly looking.

"The Merchant will meet at the prearranged place, if he manages to obtain the information he seeks," he said. He did not know where that was, nor what the information was. The Merchant had not taken him that far into his trust. It surprised him that he had been allowed knowledge of this; hired killers here on Vatch.

The man nodded as he inspected the pistol, smiled sadly, then pointed the pistol at Beck.

"Sorry," he said.

Beck tried to say something just as he became aware of the arm coming round his face from the man who had moved behind him. A grip like iron closed around his head, locked, wrenched and twisted. Beck hit the sand with his head at an angle it had never achieved in life. He made some choking sounds, shivered a little, died.

Snow halted as two proctors came in through the lock. They looked past him to the corpse on the floor. The eldest of the two, grey-bearded and running to fat, but with weapons that looked well used and well looked after, spoke to him.

"You are Snow," he said.

"Yes," Snow replied. This man was not Andronache.

"A challenge?"

"Yes."

The man nodded, looked calculatingly at the two Andronache at the bar, then turned back to the moisture-lock. It was not his job to pick up the corpses. There was an organization for that. The girl would be in a condensation jar within the hour.

"The Androche would speak with you. Come with me." To his companion he said, "Deal with it. Her two friends look like they ought to spend a little time in detention."

Snow followed the man outside.

"Why does she want to see me?" he asked as they strode down the scaffolded street.

"I didn't ask."

Any conversation ended there.

The Androche, like all in her position, had apartments up in the station she owned. The proctor led Snow to a caged spiral stair and unlocked the gate.

"She is above," was all he said. As Snow climbed the stair the gate clanged shut behind him.

The stairway ended at a moisture-lock hatch next to which depended a monitor and screen unit. Snow pressed the call button and waited. After a few moments a woman with cropped grey hair and a face that was all hard angles looked out at him.

"Yes?"

"You sent for me," said Snow.

The woman nodded and the lock on the hatch clunked open. He spun the handle and it rose on its hinge to allow him access. He climbed into a short metal-walled corridor that ended at a single panel door of imported wood. It looked like oak to Snow; very expensive. He pushed the door open and entered.

The room was filled with a fortune in antiques; a huge dining table surrounded by carved chairs. Plush eighteenth-century furniture, oil paintings on the walls, hand-woven rugs on the floor.

"Don't be too impressed. They're all copies."

The Androche approached from a drinks cabinet. She carried two glasses half filled with an amber drink. Snow studied her; she was an attractive woman. He estimated her age as somewhere between thirty-five and a hundred and ninety. Three centuries earlier the second figure would have been forty-five, but rejuvenation treatments had come a long way. She wore a simple toga-type dress over an athletic figure. At her hip she carried an antique – or replica – revolver.

"You know my name," said Snow meaningfully as he accepted the drink.

"I am Aleen," she replied to his unspoken question. Snow hardly heard her. He was relishing his first sip. "My God, whisky," he said, eventually.

"Yes," said Aleen, taking a sip from her drink then gesturing to a nearby sofa. They moved there and sat facing each other.

"Well, I'm here. What do you want?"

"Why is there a reward of twenty-five thousand shillings for your testicles?"

"Best ask the Merchant Baris that question, but I see it was rhetorical. You already know the answer."

Aleen nodded and Snow leant towards her.

"I would be glad to know the answer," he said. Aleen smiled, Snow leant back.

"There is a price," he said.

"Isn't there always? ...There is a man. He is the chief proctor here. His name is David Songrel."

"You want me to kill him."

"Of course. Isn't that what you are best at?"

Snow kept silent. Aleen lay back against the edge of the sofa then and regarded him over her drink.

"That is not all I want from you."

He turned and looked at her and at that moment she lifted her feet up onto the sofa so that he could see that she wore nothing underneath. He wondered if she shaved or if she was naturally bald in that area. Still meeting him eye to eye she dropped one leg back to the floor, reached between her legs, and began to masturbate, gently, with two fingers. Snow wondered what it was that turned her on; his white body and pink eyes? Other women had said it was almost like being made love to by an alien, or was it that he was a killer? Probably a bit of both.

"Part of the price?"

She nodded and put her glass to one side, then she slid closer to him on the sofa and hooked one leg over the back of it.

"Now," she said, reaching up and pulling apart her toga to expose breasts just like those of the girl he had killed. Snow searched himself for an adverse reaction to that, and when he found there was none he stood up and unclipped his dust robes.

"You're white as paper," said Aleen in amazement as he peeled off his under suit, and then her eyes strayed to the covered stump terminating his left arm. She said nothing about that.

"Yes," said Snow as he knelt between her legs and bowed down to run his tongue round her nipples. "A blank page," he went on as he worked his way down. She caught his head.

"Not that," she said. "I want you inside me, now."

Snow obliged her, but was puzzled at something he had heard in her voice. It had almost been as if that part of the act was the most important. Perhaps she wanted white-skinned children.

Hirald called out before approaching the fire. It had been her observation that the Andronache got rather twitchy if you walked into one of their camps unannounced. As she walked in she was surprised to see that these were not

Andronache. There were two men and two women dressed in monofilament survival suits that looked to be of Mars manufacture. Hirald noted this but pretended not to notice the weapons laid out on a groundsheet that one of the men had hastily covered at her arrival. She walked to the fire and squatted down. One of the women tossed on another crab-bird carapace and watched her through the flames. The man who had covered the weapons, a tall Marsman with caste markings tattooed on his temples, was the first to speak.

"You've come a long way?" he asked.

"Not so far as you," said Hirald. She looked from him to the woman across the flames, who also had caste marks on her face. The other couple: the man a

Negro with incongruous blue eyes and the woman Hirald thought could have come from anywhere until she noted the caps over the neural plugs behind her ears. She was corporate then; from one of the families.

"Yes, we have come a way," said the man, touching his caste mark.

"We search," said the Negro intently. "Perhaps you can help us. We search for one who is called Snow. He is an albino."

They all looked at Hirald then, avidly.

"I have heard of him," said Hirald, "and I have heard that many people look for him. I do not know where he is though."

The woman with the neural plugs looked suspicious.

Hirald continued to forestall anything more she might say.

"You are after the reward then?"

The four looked to each other, then the latter three looked to the Marsman. He smiled to himself and casually reached for the covered weapons next to him. Hirald glanced at the corporate woman, who was staring back at her.

"Jharit, no."

Jharit stopped with his hand by the covering.

"What is it, Canard Meck?"

The woman, now identified as a member of the Jethro Manx Canard corporate family, slowly shook her head then looked to Hirald, who had not yet moved.

"We have no dispute with you, but we would prefer it if you left our camp, please."

"But she knows. She might tell him," said Jharit.

Canard Meck looked to him and said, "She is product."

Jharit snatched his hand from the weapons and suddenly looked very frightened. He flinched as Hirald rose to her feet. Hirald smiled.

"I mean no harm, unless harm is meant."

She strode out into the darkness without checking behind. No one moved. No one reached for the weapons.

Snow removed the pistol from its holster in his dust robes and checked the charge reading. As was usual it was nearly at full charge. The bright sunlight of Vatch acting on the photovoltaic material of his robes kept the weapon constantly charged through the socket in the holster. The weapon was a matt black L, five millimetres thick with only a slight depression where a trigger would normally have been. It was keyed to Snow. No one else could fire it. The beam it fired was of antiphotons; a misnomer really, as what it consisted of was protons field-accelerated to the point where they became photonic matter. Misnomer or not, this beam could burn large holes in anyone Snow cared to point it at.

David Songrel was a family man. Snow had observed him lifting a child high in the air while a woman looked on from the background, just before the door to his apartments closed. Snow wondered why Aleen wanted him dead. As the owner of the water station she had much power here, but little over the proctors who enforced planetary law, not her law. Perhaps she had been involved in illegalities of which Songrel had become aware. No matter, for the present. He rapped on the door and when Songrel opened it he stuck the pistol in his face and walked him back into the apartment, closing the door behind him with his stump.

"Daddy!" the little girl yelled, but the mother caught hold of her before she rushed forward. Songrel had his hands in the air, his eyes not leaving the pistol. Shock there, knowledge.

"Why," said Snow, "does the Androche want you dead?"

"You're ... the albino."

"Answer the question please."

Songrel glanced at his wife and daughter before he replied, "She is a collector of antiquities."

"Why the necessity for your death?"

"She has killed to get what she wants. I have evidence. We intend to arrest her soon."

Snow nodded then holstered his pistol. "I thought it would be something like that. She had two proctors come for me you know."

Songrel lowered his hands, but kept them well away from the stun-gun hooked on his belt.

"As Androche she does have the right to some use of the proctors. It is our duty to guard her and her property. She does not have freedom to commit crime. Why didn't you kill me? They say you have killed many."

Snow looked to Songrel's wife and child.

"My reputation precedes me," he said, and stepped past Songrel to drop onto a comfortable-looking sofa. "But the stories are in error. I have killed no one who has not first tried to kill me... well, mostly."

Songrel looked to his wife.

"It's Tamtha's bedtime."

His wife nodded and took the child from the room. Snow noted the little girl's fascinated stare. He was quite used to such. Songrel sat himself in an armchair opposite Snow.

"A nice family you have."

"Yes... will you testify against the Androche?"

"You can have my testimony recorded under seal, but I cannot stay for a trial. If I was to stay this place would be crawling with Andronache killers in no time. I might not survive that."

Songrel nodded.

"Why did you come here if it was not your intention to kill me?" he asked, a trifle anxiously.

"I want you to play dead while I go back and see the Androche."

Songrel's expression hardened. "You want to collect your reward."

"Yes, but my reward is not money, it is information. The Androche knows why the Merchant Baris has a reward out for my death. It is a subject I am understandably curious about."

Songrel interlaced his fingers in his lap and stared down at them for a moment. When he looked up he said, "The reward is for your stasis-preserved testicles. Perhaps like Aleen he is a collector, but that is beside the point. I will play dead for you, but when you go to see Aleen I want you to carry a virtual recorder."

Snow nodded once. Songrel stood up and walked to a wall cupboard. He returned with a holocorder that he rested on the table and turned on.

"Now, your statement."

"He is dead," said Aleen, a smile on her face.

"Yes," said Snow, dropping Songrel's identity tag on the table. "Yet I get the impression you knew before I came here."

Aleen went to the drinks cabinet and poured Snow a whisky. She brought it over to him.

"I have friends amongst the proctors. As soon as his wife called in the killing – she was hysterical apparently – they informed me."

"Why did you want him killed?"

"That is none of your concern. Drink your whisky and I will get you the promised information."

Aleen turned away from him and moved to a computer console elegantly concealed in a Louis XIV table. Snow had the whisky to his lips just as his suspicious nature took over. Why was it necessary to get the information from the computer? She could just tell him. Why had she not poured a drink for herself? He placed the drink down on a table, unsampled. Aleen looked up, a dead smile on her face, and as her hand came up over the console Snow dived to one side. On the wall behind him a picture blackened then flared into oily flames. He came up on one knee and fired once. She slammed back out of her chair onto the floor, her face burning like the picture.

Snow searched hurriedly. Any time now the proctors would arrive. In the bathroom he found a device like a chrome penis with two holes in the end. One hole spurted out some kind of fluid and the other hole sucked. Some kind of contraceptive device? He traced tubes back to the unit that contained the bottle of fluid and some very complicated straining and filtering devices. To his confusion he realized it was for removing the contents of a woman's womb, probably after sex. She collected men's semen? Shortly after, he found a single stasis bottle containing said substance. It had to be his own, and now he had an inkling of an idea; a possible explanation for his situation of the last five years. He opened the bottle and washed its contents down the sink just before the proctors broke into the apartment. Not that there was very much of value in it.

Hirald looked at the man in the condensation bottle, her expression revealing nothing. He was alive beyond his time; some sadist had dropped a bottle of water in with him to prolong his suffering. He stared at Hirald with drying eyes, the empty bottle by his head, his body shrunken and badly sunburnt, his black tongue protruding. Hirald looked around carefully, there were harsh penalties for what she was about to do, then held a small chrome cylinder against the glass near the man's head. There was a brief flash. The man convulsed and the bottle was misted with smoke and steam. He died. Hirald replaced the device in her pocket, stood and walked on. Her masters would not have been pleased at her risking herself like this, but then they did not have complete control over her actions.

Snow was glad to leave the station behind him and this was reflected in his pace. He walked away at a kilometre-eating stride and occasionally swore with obscene precision. After the death of Aleen, Songrel had not felt obliged to honour his promise and Snow had spent two days in protective custody while the wheels of justice ground out slow due process. Luckily the appointment of the new Androche, traditionally a time of holiday and peace, had given him a needed respite. He had a day before the killers came after him.

Passing the condensation jar he noted that the man was now dead, his body giving up the last of its water for the public good. He paused for a moment to observe the greasy film on the inside of the jar before moving on. Someone had finished the poor bastard off. Snow wondered if that same someone might be after him, for the same purpose.

Out of sight of the station Snow left the road and set out across a spill of desert to a distant rock field. There he would be able to lose himself, if a sand shark did not get him first. He drew his pistol as he walked and kept his eyes open. One sand shark twitched its motion-detecting palps above the sand but shortly subsided. It must have fed in the last solstan year. It would be quiescent for another year to come.

Without event Snow reached the rock field and was putting away his pistol when a flash of reflected light alerted him to possible danger. Andronache, he thought, and readied himself for another challenge, only this time there was no challenge.

Automatic fire flicked his dust robes and scored pain across his ribs. Splinters from a nearby rock impacted on his mask. Snow dropped and quickly pulled himself behind a rock.

"Idiot," he said. It had been some time since anyone other than an Andronache killer had tried for him. He had forgotten that their honour code did not apply to all. He crouched down further as rock shattered above his head and rained splinters down on him.

"Hey, Snow!"

Snow did not reply.

"Hey, Snow, if you stick anything out make sure it's not worth money!"

There was laughter at this rapier wit. Two of them at least. Snow ground his teeth then pulled a couple of shiny spheroids from his belt. A volley of shots hit the rock so he supposed that at least one of them was changing position. Holding one of the spheroids to his mouth he twisted its top with his teeth then threw it hard in the general direction of the laughter. The explosion seemed completely out of proportion to the size of the object he had thrown, but then most explosives were merely matter, not field-compressed antimatter. Snow was up and running as shattered stone rained down and a great dust-cloud spread. He was behind another rock before the screams started.

"You bastard! I'll have your balls off with a blunt knife for that!"

The voice had come from that formation to the right. The screaming came from the one to the left of it. Snow fired at the first until he got a reply, two replies. There was someone else a lot closer. Three of them then, unless there were others who were more canny. He fired a few more times, rock disintegrating and fragmenting at each hit, then he checked the charge on his pistol, holstered it, and waited, listening intently. The screaming had become a steady groaning and swearing.

Sporadic firing splintered the rock between him and his antagonists. This did not disconcert Snow. He knew it was covering fire for the one who was creeping up on him. He heard the first betraying scrape of shock armour against stone shortly after one such burst of fire. It was out to his left. He drew his pistol and, pointing in that direction, waited. Then, a distraction, the groaning of the wounded man abruptly ceased.

"David! David! Answer me!"

No answer. Snow wondered if someone else had just joined the game. Thinking on this he almost missed the flicker of movement as the creeper stood up and sighted on him down the barrel of an Optek assault rifle. It was all the man had time to do. Snow fired once, his pistol on its highest setting. The man turned into an explosion of burning flesh, grisly remnants stuck to the rock and smoked.

"Oh my God! Oh you bastard!"

Snow wondered at the talker's sense of proportion. He hadn't started this. It was not his fault that they had underestimated his armament. He glanced in the direction of the rock formation the man was concealed behind and saw him come out and come running towards him. He was firing wildly, his Optek on automatic. Snow had no time to return fire. He dived for cover. Abruptly the firing stopped. Snow waited for a moment then slowly peered out from cover. The man was flat on his face, the top of his head lying about a metre in front of him. Walking towards him, an Optek resting across her shoulder, was the most beautiful woman Snow had ever seen, and he had seen a lot.

Three Optek rifles, a dilapidated laser only a fool or a desperate man would risk firing, food, aged desert survival packs and suits, a little cash money, and now useless identity tags; the sum remains of three lives. These had been poor men; staking all on one last gamble for wealth. They had tried. Snow removed what was of most value and easily transportable; the money, liquid rations, power packs and filters from the suits, and left the rest in plain sight for anyone who wanted to take it. The woman, Hirald, retained one Optek rifle and ammunition, she did not seem interested in the rest. On the other side of the rock field, away from the stink of opened bodies and the sudden interest of crab-birds and sickle flies, Snow made a fire from old carapaces and removed his mask in the light of evening. He was curious to note that the woman had not replaced her mask since the first moment he had seen her that morning, and her skin looked as clear and as perfect as it had looked then. She sank down next to him by the fire, with a grace that could only reflect superb physical condition.

"What brought you to the rock field?" he asked her.

"I made a shortcut across the Thira and was on my way back to the road and civilization, and I of course found one of the nastier aspects of this civilization."

Snow was doubtful about this reply. He had crossed the Thira a couple of times and knew it to be rough going.

Hirald looked as fresh as someone after a month's sojourn in a water station.

"I see," he said.

"You are Snow," she said, turning and fixing him with eyes that were violet in the fading light. He felt his stomach lurch at that look, then immediately felt a self-contempt, that after all these years he could still react this way to mere physical attractiveness, no, beauty.

"Yes, I am."

"I would like to travel with you for a while."

"You know who I am, then you will know at once why I am suspicious of your motives."

She smiled at him and he felt that lurch again. He turned and spat in the fire.

"I'm crossing the Thira," he said.

"I have no problem with that," she told him.

Snow lay back and rested his head on one of the packs. He pulled a thermal sheet across his body and stared up at the sky. The red-tinted swathe of stars was being encroached on by asteroids of the night. A single sword of light cut the sunset.

"Why?" he asked.

"Because I'm lonely, and after the water station I would have travelled on alone. I felt like a change."

Snow grunted in reply and closed his eyes. She was not out to kill him. He had given her ample opportunity as they crossed the rock field. But she did

have motives as yet unrevealed to him.
Whatever, she would never keep to the
pace he set and would soon abandon him,
and the unsettling things he was feeling
would soon go away. He slept.

Sunlight on his face, bringing the familiar
tingling prior to burning, had his hand
up and closing his mask across before
he was fully awake. He looked across
the dead ashes of the fire at Hirald and
got the unsettling notion that she had
not changed position all night. He sat
up, then after a muttered good morning,
went behind a rock and urinated into his
condenser pack. Following the ritual of
every morning for many years now he
then emptied the moisture collectors of

his under suit into it as well. The collector bottle he emptied into his drinking bottle before dipping his toothbrush and cleaning his teeth. By the time he had finished his ablutions and come out from behind the rock, Hirald had opened a breakfast-soup ration pack and it was bubbling under its lid. Snow reached for another pack, but she held up her hand.

"This is for you. I have already eaten."

"Did you sleep at all?"

"A little. Tell me, how is it you are in possession of proscribed weaponry?"

"Took it off someone who tried to kill me," he lied, but he could hardly tell her he had brought it here before the runcible proscription and modified it himself over the so very many years since. He sat down and drank his breakfast. When he had finished they set out across the Thira. Hirald noted him looking at her after an hour's walking and closed her mask. He thought no more of it; lots of people did not like the masks and were prepared to pay the price of water-loss not to wear them so much.

By midmorning the temperature had reached forty-five degrees and was still rising. A sand shark broke out of the surface of a dune and came scuttling after them for a few metres, then halted, panting like a dog, either too tired or too well fed to continue, that or it had sampled human flesh before and found it without nourishment. When the temperature reached fifty and the cooling units of Snow's under suit were labouring under the load, he noted that Hirald still easily matched his pace. When a crab-bird dropped clacking out of the sky at them she brought it down with one shot before Snow could even think of reaching for his weapon. She was a remarkable woman, yes, remarkable. Shortly after midday Snow called a halt.

"We'll rest until evening then continue through the night and tomorrow morning. The following night should bring us out the other side."

Hirald nodded in agreement. Snow wondered why she had not suggested this earlier. Surely she had not travelled only by day across here? Surely not.

They slept under the reflective shelter of Snow's day tent, then moved on at sunset after he had checked their position by the satellite beacons. They walked all night and most of the following morning, and when they finally set up the tent again Snow was exhausted. With a hint of irritation he told Hirald he wanted privacy in the tent and suggested she set up her own. Once inside his tent he sealed up and stripped naked. He then cleaned himself and the inside of his under suit with a cycle sponge; a device that made it possible to stay clean with a quarter-litre of water and little spillage. After this he pulled on a pair of towelling shorts and lay back with his miniature air cooler humming away at full power. It was luxury of a kind. After half an hour's sleep he woke and opened the tent to look outside. Hirald was sitting in the sand with her mask open. She was watching the horizon intently, her stillness quite unnatural.

"Don't you have a day tent?" Snow asked.

She shook her head.

"Come and join me then," he said, reversing back into his tent. Hirald stood and walked over, the effects of the baking sun seemingly negligible to her. She entered the tent and closed it behind her, then after a glance at Snow she began to remove her survival suit. Snow turned away for a moment then thought, what the hell, and turned back to watch. She had not asked him to turn his head. Under her suit she wore a single skin-hugging garment that ended above her knees and elbows and in an arc exposing perfectly formed collarbones.

The material of the garment was like white silk, and almost translucent. Snow swallowed drily, then tried to distract himself by wondering about her sanitary arrangements. As she lifted her legs up to remove her trousers from her feet he saw then how the matter was arranged and wondered if a blush was evident on his white skin. The garment had a vent from the lower part of her pale pubic hair round to the top crease of her buttocks.

As she finally took off her trousers Hirald looked at him and noted the direction of his gaze. He raised his eyes and met her eye to eye. She smiled at him and while smiling stretched the sleeves of the garment down and off over her hands and rolled it down below her breasts. Snow cleared his throat and tried to think of something witty to say. She was a succubus, a lonely desert man's fantasy. Still smiling she came across the tent on her hands and knees, put her hand against his chest and pushed him back, sat astride him, and with her pale hair falling either side of his head, leant down and kissed him on the mouth. Her mouth was sweet and warm. Snow was thoroughly aware of her hard little nipples sliding from side to side against his chest. He touched the skin of her shoulders and found it dry and warm. She sat back then and looked down at him for a moment. There was something strange about that look; a kind of cold curiosity. She slid forward onto his stomach then turned and reached back to pull his shorts down and off his legs. He was amazed at just how far she could twist and bend back her body. Once his shorts were removed she slid back until his penis rested between her buttocks then, after raising herself a little, she continued to push back, bending it over until it almost caused him pain, then with a swift movement of her pelvis, took it inside her. Snow groaned, then gritted his teeth as she started to ride him, staring down at him with that strange expression on her face.

In the evening, when it was time to move on, Snow moved with a bone-deep lethargy. He had not slept much during the afternoon. Each time he had tried to relax after a session of sex Hirald would do something, whether that would be to take his penis in her mouth or assume some position he could not resist. This had been after her climax while she rode him. It had been so intense that she had cried out and shuddered uncontrollably, and after it she had looked down at herself in surprise and shock. Thereafter she had been eager to repeat the experience. Snow felt sore and drained.

As they walked across the darkened violet sands they had talked little, but there had been one conversation that had raised Snow's suspicions.

"Your hand, how did you lose it?"

"Andronache challenge. It was shredded by a flack shell."

"How is it now?"

Snow had paused before replying. Did she know?

"What do you mean; how is it? It was amputated. It is no longer there."

"Yes," she had said, and no more.

The sun was breaking the horizon and the night asteroids fading out of the sky when they reached the rock field at the edge of the Thira. With little energy to spare for conversation, Snow set up his day tent and collapsed inside, instantly asleep. When he woke in the latter part of the day it was to discover himself undressed under a blanket with Hirald lying beside him. She was up on her elbow, her head propped on her hand, looking at his face. As soon as she saw that he was awake she handed him a carton of mixed juice. He sat up, the blanket sliding down. She was naked. He drank the juice.

"I'm glad you came along," he said, and the rest of the day was spent in pleasant activity. That night they moved deep into the rock field. The following day passed much as the one before.

"I think it fair to tell you I have an implant," Snow said as he rested after some particularly vigorous activity. "You won't get pregnant by me, and my sperm is little more than water and a few free proteins."

"Why do you feel it necessary to tell me this?" Hirald asked him.

"As you know, there is a reward out for my testicles, stasis-preserved. This is not because the Merchant Baris particularly wants me dead. I think it is because he is after my genetic tissue. It has value, of a kind. At the water station the Androche ... seduced me." Snow was uncomfortable with that. "She did it so she could collect my sperm, probably to sell."

"I know," said Hirald. Snow looked at her and she went on, "He is after your testicles to provide him with an endless supply of your genetic material."

Snow considered that. Of course there had to be more to Hirald than he had supposed, but the Olympic screwing had clouded his thought-processes somewhat.

"He wouldn't get that ... meiosis only leaves half the chromosomes in each sperm," he said.

"He would get there eventually. Your testicles could be kept alive and producing spermatozoa for a very long time. It is the next best thing to having your entire living body to provide the genetic material. I suspect Baris thought it unlikely he could get away with that. He'd never get you off-planet without your consent. This way he also corners the market."

"You know an awful lot about what Baris wants."

Hirald looked at him very directly.

"How is your hand?"

Snow looked down at the stump. He unclipped the covering and pulled it off.

What he exposed was recognizably a hand, though deformed and almost useless. The covering had been cleverly made to conceal it, to make it look as if the hand was missing.

"It will be no different from its predecessor in about six solstan months. I intended to walk out of one water station without a hand, then into another station with a hand and a new identity."

"What about your albinism?"

"Skin dye and eye lenses."

"Of course you cannot take transplants."

"No ... I think you should explain yourself."

"The people I work for want the same as Baris; your genome."

"You've had opportunity ..."

"No, they want the best option; you, willingly. I want you to gate back to Earth with me."

"Why?"

"You are regenerative. It is the source of your immortality. We know this now. You have known it for more than a thousand years."

"Still, why?"

"We have managed to keep your secret for the last three hundred years, ever since it was discovered. Ten years ago a mistake was made and the knowledge was leaked. Now many organizations know about you, and what you represent; whoever can decode your genome has access to immortality, and through that, access to wealth and power unprecedented. Baris is one who would like this. He was the first to track you down. There will be others."

"You work for Earth Central."

"Yes."

"Wouldn't it be better just to kill me and destroy my body?"

"Earth Central does not suppress knowledge." Hirald smiled at him. "You should be old enough to understand the futility of this. It wants this knowledge disseminated so that it cannot cause damage, cannot put power into the hands of the wrong people. The good it would do is immense also. The projections are that in ten years a treatment could become available to make anyone regenerative, within limits."

"Yet till now it kept a lid on things," said Snow, an old hand at spotting discrepancies like this.

"It guarded your privacy. It did not suppress knowledge. Not suppressing knowledge is not equal to seeking it out."

"Is Earth Central so moral now?" wondered Snow, then could have kicked himself for the stupidity. Of course Earth Central was. Only human beings and other low-grade sentients could become corrupt, and Earth Central was the most powerful AI in the human polity. Hirald, noting his discomfiture, did not answer his question.

"Will you come?" she asked him.

Snow looked to the wall of the tent as if looking out across the rock field.

"This requires thought, not instant decisions. Two days should bring us to my home. I will... consider."

Draped in chameleon cloth the hover transport was indistinguishable from the surrounding dunes. Inside the transport Jharit shuffled a pack of cards and played a game men like him had played in similar situations for many centuries. His wife, Jharilla, slept. Trock was cleaning an antique revolver he had picked up in an auction at the last water station. The bullets he had acquired with it stood in neat soldierly rows on the table before him. Canard Meck was plugged in, trying to pick up information from the net and the high-speed conversations the runcible AI had with its subminds. The call came as a relief to all of them but her; she resented dropping out of that world of perfect logic and pure clarity of thought back into the sweat-stink of the transport.

"I am Baris," said the smiling face from the screen.

Coming straight to the point Jharit said, "You have the information?"

"I have," said Baris, his smile only slightly less, "and I will be coming to join you for the final chase."

Jharit and Trock exchanged a look. "As you wish. You are paying."

"Yes, I am." The Merchant's smile was gone now. "Turn on your beacon and I will join you within the hour."

"How are you getting out here?" asked Canard Meck.

"By AGC of course," said Baris, turning to look towards her.

"All AGCs are registered. The AI will know where you are."

Baris flicked his fingers at this and his face assumed a look of contempt.

"No matter. We will continue from your position to ... our destination, in the transport."

"Very well," said Canard Meck.

Baris waited for something more to be said, and when nothing was he gave a moue of disappointment. The screen blanked.

The Merchant arrived in a fancy repro Macrojet AGC. He climbed out dressed in sand fatigues and was followed by two women dressed much the same. One of them carried a hunting rifle and ammunition belts. The other carried various unidentifiable packages. Baris struck a pose before them. He was a handsome man. Not one of the four reacted to this foolish display. They knew that anyone who had reached the Merchant's position was no fool. Jharit and Jharilla looked at him glassy eyed. Trock looked at the rifle. Canard Meck looked briefly at one of the women, took in the imbecilic smile, then back to the Merchant.

"Shall we be on our way then?" she said.

Baris shook his head and still smiling he clicked his fingers and walked to the transport. The two women followed him as obediently as dogs. The four came after: hounds of a different breed.

Out of the rock field reared the first of the stone buttes, carved by wind-blown sand to resemble a statue of something manlike sunk up to its chest in the ground. In the cracks and divisions of its head, mica and quartz glittered like insectile eyes. Snow led the way to the base of the butte where slabs of the same stone lay tilted in the ground.

"Here," he said, holding his hand out to a sandwich of slabs. With a grinding, the top slab pivoted to one side to expose a stair dropping a short distance to the floor of a tunnel. "Welcome to my home."

"You live in a hole in the ground?" said Hirald with a touch of irony.

"Come and find out."

As they climbed down the slab swung back across above them and wall lights clicked on. Hirald noted that the tunnel led under the butte and had already worked things out by the time they reached the chimney with its rails pinned up the side and the elevator car. They climbed inside the car and sprawled in the seats ringing the inside, looked out of the windows as it hauled them up the chimney cut through the centre of the butte.

"This must have taken you some time," said Hirald.

Snow said, "The shaft was already here. About two hundred years ago I first found it. Others had lived here before me, but in rather primitive conditions. I've been improving the place ever since."

The car arrived at its destination and they walked from it into a complex of moisture-locked rooms at the head of the butte. With a drink in her hand Hirald stood at a polarized panoramic window and looked out across the rock field for a moment, then returned her attention to the room and its contents. In a glass-fronted case along one wall was a display of weapons dating from the twenty-second century and at the centre of this a sword dating from some prespace age. Hirald had to wonder. She turned from the case as Snow returned to the room, dressed now in loose black trousers and a black open-necked shirt. The contrast with his white skin and hair and pink eyes gave him the appearance of someone who might have a taste for blood.

"There's some clothing there for you to use if you like, and the shower. No problem with it cycling. There's plenty of water here," he told her. Hirald nodded, placed her drink down on a glass-topped table, and headed back into the rooms Snow had come from. Snow watched her go. She would shower and change and be little fresher than she already was. He had noted with some puzzlement how she never seemed to smell bad, never seemed dirty.

"Whose clothing is this?" Hirald asked from the room beyond.

"My last wife's," said Snow.

Hirald came to the door with clothing folded over one arm. She looked at him questioningly.

"She killed herself about a century ago," he said in a flat voice. "Walked out into the desert and burnt a hole through her head. I found her before the crab-birds and sand sharks."

"Why?"

"She grew old and I did not. She hated it."

Hirald had no comment to make on this. She went to take her shower, and shortly returned wearing a skin-tight body suit of translucent blue material, which she did not expect to be wearing for long once Snow saw her in it. Snow was occupied though; sat in a swivel chair looking at a screen, he was back in his dust robes, his terrapin mask hanging open. She walked up behind him to see what he was looking at. She saw the hover transport on the sand and the two women pulling a sheet over it. The Merchant Baris she recognized, as she recognized the four hired killers.

"It would seem Baris has found me," said Snow, his tone cold and flat.

"What defences does this place have?"

"None, I never felt the need for them."

"Are you sure they are coming here?"

"It seems strange that he has chosen this particular rock field on the whole planet. I'll have to go and settle this."

"I'll change," said Hirald, and hurried back to get her suit. When she returned

Snow was gone. When she tried to follow she found the elevator car locked at the bottom of the shaft.

"Damn you Snow!" she yelled, slamming her fist against a doorjamb, leaving a fist-shaped dent in the steel. She then walked back a few paces, turned, and ran and leapt into the shaft. The rails pinned to the edge were six metres away. She reached them easily, her hands locking on the polished metal with a thump. Laboriously she began to climb down.

Jharit smiled at his wife and nodded to Trock, who stood beyond her strapping on body armour. This was the one. They would be rich after this. He looked at the narrow-beam laser he held. He would have preferred something with a little more power, but it was essential that the body not be too badly damaged. He turned to Baris as the Merchant sent his two women back to the transport.

"We'll go in spread out. He probably has scanning equipment in the rock field and if there's an ambush we don't want him to get too many of us at once."

Baris smiled and thumbed bullets into his rifle, adjusted the scope. Jharit wondered about him, wondered how good he was. He gave the signal; they spread out and entered the rock field.

They were coming to kill him. There were no rules, no challenges offered. Snow braced the butt of his pistol against the rock and sighted along it.

"Anything?" asked Jharit over the com.

"Pin cameras," Jharilla told him. "I burnt a couple out, but there has to be more. He knows we're here."

"Me too," said Trock.

"Remember, narrow beam. We burn too much and there's no money. A clean kill. A head shot would be nice."

There was a whooshing sound, a brief scream, static over the com. Jharit hit the ground and moved behind a rock.

"What the hell was that?"

"He's got a fucking APW! Fucking body armour's useless!"

Jharit felt a sinking sensation in his gut. They had expected projectile weapons, perhaps a laser.

"Who ...?"

There was a pause.

"Trock?"

"Jharilla's dead."

Jharit swallowed drily and edged on into the rock field.

"Position?"

"Don't know."

"Meck?"

"Nothing here."

"Baris?"

There was no reply from the Merchant.

Snow dropped down off the top of the boulder and pulled the remaining two spheroids from his belt. With his teeth he twisted their tops right round. The dark-skinned one was over to his left. The Marsman over to his right. The others were further over to the right somewhere. He threw the two spheroids right and left and moved back then flicked through multiple views on his wrist screen. A lot of the cameras were out, but he pulled up a view of the Marsman. Two detonations. As the Marsman hit the ground he realized he had thrown too far there. He was close. He flicked through the views again and caught the other stumbling through dust and wreckage, rock splinters embedded in his face. Ah, so. Snow moved to his left, checking his screen every few seconds. He halted behind a tilted slab and after checking his screen once more he squatted down and waited. With little regard for his surroundings Trock stumbled out of the falling dust. Snow smiled grimly under his mask and sighted on him. Red agony cut his shoulder. The smell of burning flesh. Snow rolled to one side, came up onto his feet, ran. Rock to one side of him smoked, pinged as it heated. He dived for cover, crawled amongst broken rock. The firing ceased. Now I'm dead, he thought. His pistol lay in the dust back there somewhere.

"He dropped the APW, Trock. He's over to your left. Take him down, I can't get a sighting at the moment."

Trock spat a broken tooth from his mouth and walked in the direction indicated, his antique revolver in his left hand and his laser in his right. This was it. The bastard was dead, or perhaps not. I'll cut his arms and legs off, the beam should cauterize sufficiently. Trock did not get time to fire. The figure in dust robes came out of nowhere to drop-kick him in the chest. The body armour absorbed most of the blow, but Trock went over. Before he could rise the figure was above him. A split-hand blow drove through his visor and deep into his eyes, two fingers each, and burst them. It was a strike Snow had learnt over a thousand years before. By the time Trock started screaming and firing Snow was gone again.

Snow coughed as quietly as he could, opened his mask and spat out a mixture of bloody plasma and charred tissue. The burn had started at his shoulder and penetrated his left lung. A second more and he would have been dead. The pain was crippling. He knew he would not have the energy for another attack like that, nor would he be likely to take any of the others by surprise. The man had been stunned by the explosion, angered by the injuries to himself. Snow edged back through the rock field, his mobility rapidly decreasing. When a shadow fell across him he looked up into the inevitable.

"Why didn't you take his weapon?" asked Jharit, nodding back in the direction of Trock, who was no longer screaming. He was curled foetal by a rock, a field dressing across his eyes and his body pumped full of self-administered painkillers.

"No time, no strength ... could only get him through his visor," Snow managed.

Jharit nodded and spoke into his com.

"I have him. Home in on my signal."

Snow waited for death, but Jharit squatted in the dust by him seemingly disinclined to kill him.

"Jharilla was a hell of a woman," said Jharit, removing a stasis bottle from his belt and pushing it into the sand next to him. "We were married in Viking City twenty solstan years ago." Jharit pulled a wicked ceramal knife from his boot and held it up before his face. "This is for her you understand. After I've taken your testicles and dressed that wound I'll see to your other injury. I don't want you to die yet. I have so much to tell you about her, and there is so much I want you to experience. You know she—"

Jharit turned at a sound, rose to his feet and drew his laser again. He stepped away from Snow and looked around. Snow looked beyond him but could see nothing.

"If you leave here now, Marsman, I will not kill you."

The voice was Hirald's.

Jharit fired into the rocks and backed towards Snow. "I have a singun and I am in chameleonwear. I can kill you any time I wish. Drop your weapon."

Jharit paused for a moment as if indecisive, then he whirled, pointing his laser at Snow. The expression on his face told all. Before he could press the trigger he collapsed into himself; a central point the size of a pinhead, a plume of sand standing where he stood, then all blasted away in a thunderclap and an encore of miniature lightnings across the ground. Snow slowly shoved himself to his feet as he looked in awe at the spot Jharit had occupied. He had heard of such weapons and not believed. He looked across as Hirald flickered back into existence only a few metres away. She smiled at him, just before the first shot ripped the side of her face away.

Snow knew he yelled, he might have screamed. He looked on in impotent horror as the second shot smacked into her back and knocked her to the ground. Then there: Baris and the corporation woman, walking out of the rock field. Baris sighted again as he walked, hit Hirald with another shot that ripped half her side away. Snow felt his legs give way. He went down on his knees. Baris came before him, a self-satisfied smirk on his face. Snow looked up at him, trying to pull the energy together to throw it all in one attempt. He knew it was what Baris was waiting for. It was all he could do. He glanced aside at the woman, saw she had halted some way back. She was looking past Baris at Hirald, a look of horror on her face. Snow did not want to look. He did not want to know.

"Oh my God. It's her!"

Snow pulled himself to his feet, dizziness making him lurch. Baris grinned and pointed the rifle at his face, relished his moment for the half a second it lasted. The hand punched through his body, knocked the rifle aside, lifted him and hurled him against a rock with such force he stuck for a moment, then fell leaving a man-shaped corona of blood. Hirald stood there, revealed. Where the syntheflesh had been blown away glittering ceramal was exposed, her white enamel teeth, one blue eye complete in its socket, the ribbed column of her spine.

She observed Snow for a moment then turned towards the woman. Snow fainted before the scream.

He was in his bed and memories slowly dragged themselves into his mind. He lay there, his throat dry, and after a moment felt across to his numbed shoulder and the dressing. It was a moment before he dared open his eyes. Hirald sat at the side of the bed, and when she saw he was awake she helped him up into a sitting position against his pillows. Snow observed her face. She had repaired the damage somehow, but the scars of that repair work were still there. She looked just like a human woman who had been disfigured in an accident. She wore a loose shirt and trousers to hide the other repairs. As he looked at her she reached up and self-consciously touched her face, before reaching for a glass of water to hand to him. Gratefully he drained the glass, that touch of vanity confusing him for a moment.

"You're a Golem android," he said, in the end, unsure.

Hirald smiled and it did not look so bad.

She said, "Canard Meck thought that." When she saw his confusion she explained, "The corporation woman. She called me product, which is an understandable mistake. I am nearly indistinguishable from the Golem Twenty-two."

"What are you then?" Snow asked as she poured him another glass of water.

"Cyborg. Underneath this syntheflesh I am ceramal. In the ceramal a human brain, spinal column, and other nerve tissues."

Snow sipped his drink as he considered that. He was not sure what he was feeling, but it certainly was not the horror he had first felt.

"Will you come to Earth with me?"

Snow turned and looked at her for a long time. He remembered how it had been in the tents as she, he realized, discovered that she was still human.

"You know, I will never grow old and die," she said.

"I know."

She tilted her head questioningly and awaited his answer. A slow smile spread across his face.

"I'll come with you," he told her. "If you will stay with me." He put his drink down and reached out to take hold of her hand. What defined humanity? There was blood still under her fingernails and the tear duct in her left eye was not working properly. It didn't matter.

# About the Author

Neal Asher was born 1961 in Billericay, Essex, the son of a school teacher and a lecturer in applied mathematics who were also SF aficionados.

Neal has had over 20 novels published and numerous short stories. The majority of his novels are set within one future history, known as the Polity universe. The Polity encompasses many classic science fiction tropes including world-ruling artificial intelligences, androids, hive minds and aliens.

# Also by Neal Asher

*Agent Cormac series*

Gridlinked
The Line of Polity Brass Man
Polity Agent
Line War

*Spatterjay trilogy*

The Skinner
The Voyage of the Sable Keech
Orbus

*Polity standalone novels*

Prador Moon
Hilldiggers Shadow of the Scorpion
The Technician

*The Owner trilogy*

The Departure
Zero Point
Jupiter War

*Transformation trilogy*

Dark Intelligence
War Factory
Infinity Engine

*Rise of the Jain trilogy*

The Soldier
The Warship
The Human Cowl

*Novellas*

The Parasite
Mindgames: Fool's Mate

*Short-story collections*

Runcible Tales
The Engineer
The Gabble

**More dyslexic friendly titles coming soon...**

Milton Keynes UK
Ingram Content Group UK Ltd.
UKHW022236130624
444101UK00005BA/96